Who's Got Spots?

by Linda Williams Aber
Illustrated by Gioia Fiammenghi

The Kane Press
New York

To three special cousins,
Sophie, Chloe, and Madison
—L.A.

Book Design/Art Direction: Roberta Pressel

Library of Congress Cataloging-in-Publication Data

Aber, Linda Williams.
    Who's got spots?/by Linda Williams Aber; illustrated by Gioia Fiammenghi.
      p.   cm. — (Math matters.)
    Summary: When some classmates come down with chicken pox, Kip uses tables and
charts to help determine if there will be enough students to put on the planned Holiday Show..
    ISBN 1-57565-099-1 (pbk. : alk. paper)
    [1. Graphic methods—Fiction. 2. Chicken pox—Fiction. 3. Schools—Fiction.]
I. Fiammenghi, Gioia, ill. II. Title. III. Series.
    PZ7.A1613 Wh 2000
    [E]—dc21   99-088841
                                                                                  CIP
                                                                                   AC

10 9 8 7 6 5 4 3 2 1

First published in the United States of America in 2000 by The Kane Press.
Printed in Hong Kong.

MATH MATTERS is a registered trademark of The Kane Press.

"Good luck!" called Kip's dad.

This was the day Ms. Beck was going to announce the solo singer for the Autumn Fest. Kip was hoping it would be him.

3

Kip could hardly sit still. He was too excited. He was also worried. What if Ms. Beck stood up in front of the whole class and said someone else's name? What if the name she called was . . .

LOST KEY

DON'T FORGET
MATH QUIZ
ON
FRIDAY.

Autumn Fest

"Kip!" Ms. Beck announced with a big smile. "Kip will be our solo singer!"

All the kids cheered. For the first time since tryouts, Kip relaxed. What a great day this was turning out to be!

Practice for the Autumn Fest began right away. "It takes many voices to make a chorus," said Ms. Beck. "Kip will sing the solo, but each one of you is important. So be sure to come to every practice."

"Don't worry," said Kip. He was sure that nothing would get in the way of their show.

But the next day Kip found out that something *was* getting in the way . . .

"I have bad news," said Ms. Beck. "Three people in the chorus have chicken pox—Travis, Mai and Cory."

All the kids began talking at once. "Have you had it?...I've had it already...Will I get it?...Do you get chicken pox from a chicken?"

"A chicken? Oh, no!" said Ms. Beck.
"You catch it from someone who has it.
The good news is that once you get
chicken pox, you can never get it again."

Still, the room buzzed with worried
voices.

"What about the show?" cried Kip.

"Well, let's see," Ms. Beck said. "There are fifteen people in our chorus. We can perform if at least ten are well by the date of the show."

"What are the chances of that?" whispered Alice, the girl next to Kip. "Chicken pox is really contagious!"

"I know," said Kip in a worried voice.

Ms. Beck sighed, "All we can do is wait and see. Who knows what will happen in the next two weeks?"

"Waiting won't take the worry away,"
Kip said to Alice on the way home from
school. "I wish I could figure out what the
chances are for ten of us to be well on the
day of the show."

"Ha!" Alice laughed. "Do you have a
crystal ball that tells about chicken pox?"

A smile spread across Kip's face. "I'll talk to you later," he said. "I'm going home now to make something that will tell us more than a crystal ball. I'm going to make a chart!"

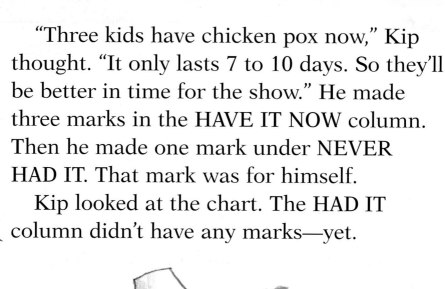

"Three kids have chicken pox now," Kip thought. "It only lasts 7 to 10 days. So they'll be better in time for the show." He made three marks in the HAVE IT NOW column. Then he made one mark under NEVER HAD IT. That mark was for himself.

Kip looked at the chart. The HAD IT column didn't have any marks—yet.

"Eleven kids to call!" he said. "Better get started!"

Kip called Alice first. "I'm doing a Chicken Pox Survey," he told her. "Have you had it?"

"I had it last year," Alice said. "You went trick-or-treating for me because I couldn't go out, remember?"

"That's right!" Kip said. He marked his chart.

Kip made more calls.
Everyone had something
different to say.

"I had it," Jim said.
"I was scratching the
whole time I was away
at camp!"

"I'll shut the doors and turn
the locks. I'll never get the
chicken pox!" rhymed Kelly.

"Chicken pox! I had 219 spots!" wailed Anna.

"My mom made me wear mittens so I wouldn't scratch," Matt told him.

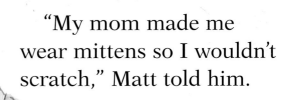

Kip called Sophie and Chloe next. Neither of them had had chicken pox. "Two more in the NEVER HAD IT column," he thought. "Only four more calls to make."

The next day Kip showed the chart to the class. "Look," he said. "We have seven kids for the show."

"How do you figure that?" asked Rob.

"Like this," explained Kip. "Four kids had chicken pox already, so they can't get it again. The three kids who have it now should be better in plenty of time to sing. That's seven kids. All we need is ten."

"I get it," said Amy. "So at least three more of us have to stay healthy!"

From that second on, everyone who had never had chicken pox tried everything NOT to get chicken pox.

Amy started wearing a mask she got from a doctor's office. "Don't breathe on me!" she said to everyone.

Fred wore gloves all day! "A glove a day keeps the germs away!" he said.

Jackson sprayed germ-killer on the chairs in the classroom. "Just to be extra safe," he whispered.

And Kip tried very hard to sing with his mouth closed! "To protect my throat," he mumbled.

The next day Chloe, Fred and Sophie were absent. "Chicken pox," Ms. Beck said sadly. "But Travis, Mai and Cory will be back tomorrow."

"Uh, oh," said Kip. "My chart doesn't work so well anymore. I can't keep track of who's sick and who isn't."

"How about making a graph with the kids' names on it?" Alice suggested. "We can use sticky notes."

"Great idea!" said Kip. "Then we can move them around if things change."

"Whew!" Kip said when they were
finished. "It's two days till the show.
If nobody else gets sick, we'll have
twelve kids."

The day before the show Ms. Beck had
some more bad news. "Kelly and Jackson,"
she said, shaking her head. "Chicken pox!"

"Oh, no!" Kip thought. "We're down to ten!" He turned to Rob and Amy. "Okay, you guys. None of us can get sick!"

That night Kip made a terrible discovery. When he took off his shirt, he looked at his stomach and gasped. "Oh, no! I've got a spot!"

Kip felt like crying. "I *have* to be in the show!" he thought. "I just won't tell anyone."

Kip crawled under the covers. In the darkness he thought about his solo. He didn't feel good about it anymore. And he knew why.

Kip sat up and shouted, "Mom, Dad!
I have chicken pox!"

His parents hurried into his room and
turned on the light. Kip showed them
the spot. Dad looked closely, and then he
laughed. "You don't have chicken pox,"
he said. "That spot's just a freckle!"

And the next spot Kip saw was the spotlight shining on him as he sang his solo—perfectly!

ORGANIZING DATA CHART

Amy and Fred took a *survey*. They asked some friends this question.

Would you sing a solo in the next show?
Then they showed the results of their survey.

Use the tally chart or the graph. Tell why each sentence is true.

1. Amy and Fred asked eleven friends.

2. More friends said "Yes" than said "No."

3. Rob said "No."

4. Chloe said "Maybe."

5. Eight friends might sing a solo in the next show.